THIS BOOK BELONGS TO:

_____

_____

_____

meomi

WOULD LIKE TO DEDICATE THIS BOOK TO OCTO-FANS AROUND THE WORLD AND HERMIT CRABS WITH ANEMONE HATS

Copyright © 2009 Meomi Design Inc. : Vicki Wong & Michael C. Murphy
First hardcover edition published 2009.

immedium
Immedium, Inc., P.O. Box 31846, San Francisco, CA 94131 www.immedium.com

This book was typeset with Rosewood, Usherwood, and hand-drawn Meomi alphabet.
For inspiration, many photos of baby sloths were perused.

Edited by Don Menn
Design by Meomi and Stefanie Liang

Printed in Malaysia. Fourth Printing: December 2013.
10 9 8 7 6 5 4

Library of Congress Cataloging-in-Publication Data

Meomi (Firm)
  The Octonauts and the great ghost reef / by Meomi. -- 1st hardcover ed.
      p. cm.
  Summary: When the Octonauts, a team of eight animals who explore the ocean,
discover a bleached and abandoned coral reef, they learn about the important relationships
among animals, plants, and their habitats.
    ISBN-13: 978-1-59702-019-0 (hardcover) ISBN-10: 1-59702-019-2 (hardcover)
    [1. Underwater exploration--Fiction. 2. Coral reefs and islands--Fiction.
    3. Coral reef ecology--Fiction. 4. Ecology--Fiction. 5. Animals--Fiction.]
I. Title.
  PZ7.M5322Op 2009
  [Fic]--dc22

                                          2009018910

Ghosts need friends, too.

THE OCTONAUTS

& the Great Ghost Reef

• MEOMI •

Immedium, Inc. • San Francisco

It was a clear and sunny day under the tropical sea when...

Captain Barnacles Bear was testing his snorkel.

Peso Penguin was shampooing Clawdius.

Tunip the Vegimal was packing a picnic basket.

Dashi Dog was picking out sunglasses.

Tweak Bunny was changing a spark plug.

Dr. Shellington was modelling his new swimsuit.

Kwazii Kitten was taking a catnap.

Professor Inkling was studying his travel guide.

REEF madness

The crew quickly assembled in the Octopod's headquarters to find Professor Inkling frantically pointing to the eerie landscape outside.

"Octonauts!" the small Dumbo octopus exclaimed. "We're all excited about our vacation to the Great Reef City, but something peculiar has transpired."

"Well, shiver me timbers – everything is white," Kwazii puzzled out loud. "This place looks like a ghost town!"

"This city is built on top of a giant coral reef. Normally reefs look like colorful rocks where many plants and animals make their homes," Dr. Shellington informed the crew. "This is not at all what I expected!"

"We need to find out what happened here," Captain Barnacles decided.

The crew cautiously explored the silent streets of the city.
As they passed abandoned buildings and empty houses,
they caught glimpses of pale shapes and heard strange creaks and moans.

"I'm sure there's a perfectly good scientific explanation for all this!" Shellington said nervously.

Eventually, they came upon an old turtle nudging a large trunk out his front door.
Noticing the name on the mailbox, Barnacles politely asked,
"Excuse me, Mr. Slowstache? Could you tell us what happened here?"
The turtle slowly looked the polar bear up and down, then gave a low sigh.

"I'm afraid it's all a great mystery." Mr. Slowstache began his tale.

"When I first moved here as a young whippersnapper, the reef was famous for its bright colors and seagrass aplenty to eat.

As time went by, more and more animals came here to live. They built fancy buildings, theaters, and shops. This place was quite the hot spot!

I guess everyone was so busy that no one noticed the coral beneath the city had started turning white and brittle. Bit by bit it spread…"

The turtle gestured sadly to his own home. "Now, even my house is falling over!"

"Nobody knows what caused this. Some even say the city is haunted!! I'm the last to go – it's just too cold here for my old bones."

Dashi patted the turtle's shell and asked, "Is there anything we can do to help?"

Mr. Slowstache smiled in appreciation. "Thank you, young lady. I remember
a beach from my childhood just two shakes of a turtle's tail from here.
I could certainly use a hand moving my rock collection there."

The Octonauts packed Mr. Slowstache's belongings onto
the Gup-A, and the ship took off with a big SWOOSH.

Arriving at the sandy dunes of the beach, Barnacles looked around and smiled,
"It sure is nice and warm — everyone seems to be enjoying the sun."

sunflower starfish

mussel beach

limpet

barnacle

sunbathing sea lion

clam holes

sea urchin

"I forgot how shallow the water is here.
An old turtle like me needs more shelter,"
Mr. Slowstache fretted as he tucked into his shell. "Let's keep looking."

nd dollars

starfish beach party

kingfisher

pelican

anemone hat shop

vegetarian boiga

mud lobster towers

saltwater crocodile

crab clean-up crew

catfish kitchen

"How about this mangrove forest?" Dashi asked.
"The trees give cover to the animals and even drop fruit down for food."

flying fox

sleepy sloth

great egret

fish grooming

mudskipper

Shaking his head stubbornly, the turtle persisted,
"But I don't see any of my favorite seagrass!"

possum

"Luckily, seagrass meadows grow right near mangroves," Peso announced cheerfully. "Look at those happy dugongs tending the fields."

bandicoot

banjo ray

fish nurseries

pipefish

fiddler crab

seagrass band audience

komodo dragon

black swan

cuttlefish

lawn mowing dugong

"The water is so murky here... not clean and clear like my old reef," fussed the turtle.

"Arrr, he sure is picky — I need a vacation from this vacation!" Kwazii muttered.

Flipping his tail in frustration, Slowstache lamented, "I never realized how special my reef was until now. There's no other place quite like it!"

"If we can't find you a new home, we'll just have to figure out what's wrong with your old one," Barnacles said confidently. "Let's head back and solve this ghost reef mystery."

Returning to the city, the crew found Tweak
using the Gup-D to prop up a row of teetering buildings.

"Watch out!" the bunny shouted out with concern.
"The city is starting to fall. We need to do something fast!"

Just then, Shellington ran up to
the crew and exclaimed,
"Octonauts — while you were away,
I discovered something very fascinating!!
The reef isn't rock at all.
It's made up of thousands
of little creatures."

THE CORAL
IS ALIVE!!

"Does that mean they're not ghosts?"
Peso timidly asked.

Shellington shook his head and explained, "No, but they are cold and hungry. When I was studying the healthy reef outside of town, I learned that each coral has algae inside that give it color and help it make food."

"Algae are plants, and plants need light," Inkling added. "The buildings must be blocking out the sun, and causing this coral to give up its algae."

"So that's why the reef turned white. Octonauts, we have to move these buildings!" Barnacles declared.

AH-HA!

News of the Octonauts' discovery spread quickly and animals from far and wide returned to help. Together, they lifted off pieces of city to uncover the coral beneath.

Everyone worked to build new homes *around* the coral instead of on top.
Slowly, the reef became colorful and healthy again.

CORAL?

PURPLE

BLUE

PINK

"Thank you for solving this mystery — now I've learned that
we need to care for the reef just like it cares for us."
The turtle gratefully presented each of the crew
with a rock from his prized collection.
"For all your HARD work!" Slowstache added, with a wink.

SLOWSTACHE

The Octonauts laughed, and all agreed this was the greatest reef vacation ever!

THE OCTONAUTS

CAPTAIN BARNACLES

Captain Barnacles is a brave polar bear extraordinaire and the leader of the Octonauts crew. He's always the first to rush in and help whenever there's a problem. In addition to adventuring, Barnacles enjoys playing his accordion and writing in his captain's log.

PESO PENGUIN

Peso is the medic for the team. He's an expert at bandaging and always carries his medical kit with him in case of emergencies. He's not too fond of scary things, but if a creature is hurt or in danger, Peso can be the bravest Octonaut of all!

TWEAK BUNNY

Tweak is the engineer for the Octopod. She keeps everything working in the launch bay and maintains the Octonauts' subs: GUP-A to GUP-E. Tweak likes all kinds of machinery and enjoys tinkering with strange contraptions that sometimes work in unexpected ways.

DOCTOR SHELLINGTON

Dr. Shellington is a nerdy sea otter scientist who loves doing field research and working in his lab. He's easily distracted by rare plants and animals, but his knowledge of the ocean is a big help in Octonaut missions.

KWAZII KITTEN

Kwazii is a daredevil orange kitten with a mysterious pirate past. He loves excitement and traveling to exotic places. His favorite pastimes include long baths, racing the Gup-B, and general swashbuckling.

DASHI DOG

Dashi is a sweet dachshund who oversees operations in the Octopod HQ and launch bay. She monitors the computers and manages all ship traffic. She's also the Octonauts' official photographer and enjoys taking photos of undersea life.

PROFESSOR INKLING

Professor Inkling is a brilliant, Dumbo octopus oceanographer. He founded the Octonauts with the intention of furthering underwater research and preservation. Because of his delicate, big brain, he prefers to help the team from his library in the Octopod.

TUNIP THE VEGIMAL

Tunip is one of many Vegimals, a special sea creature that's part vegetable and part animal, that help out around the Octopod. They speak their own language that only Shellington can understand (sometimes!). Vegimals love to bake kelp cakes, kelp cookies, kelp soufflé...